Littlest Pet Shop™

BEST FRIENDS

by Quinlan B. Lee
illustrated by Jim Talbot

SCHOLASTIC INC.

New York   Toronto   London   Auckland   Sydney
Mexico City   New Delhi   Hong Kong   Buenos Aires

ISBN 0-439-88776-3

Littlest Pet Shop © 2006 Hasbro.
LITTLEST PET SHOP and all related characters and elements are trademarks of and © Hasbro. All Rights Reserved.

Published by Scholastic Inc. SCHOLASTIC and associated logos are trademarks and/or registered trademarks of Scholastic Inc.

12 11 10 9 8 7   7 8 9 10/0

Printed in the U.S.A.
First printing, September 2006

Best friends come in all shapes and sizes. You may not look the same on the outside, but on the inside, best friends always have a lot in common. Your best friend is your closest pal.

The best thing about a best friend is having someone to play with.

It doesn't matter what you do as long as you're together!

Best friends find ways to keep in touch, even if they aren't in the same place. It might be a quick call or a long letter.

It only takes a sec to send your friend an e-mail or draw her a funny picture, but the happy feeling it gives her will last all day long!

A best friend makes getting there half the fun!

When you're traveling around town, it's always more fun if you catch a ride with your best friend.

When you're shopping with your best friend, anything goes. If your doggy bag is a little low on funds, pressing your nose against the glass and window-shopping is just as much fun!

Just being with a friend is better than anything money can buy, and being with a best friend is priceless.

Best friends always have something to celebrate—whether it's a birthday, a holiday, or just being together.

All you need are tunes, treats, and a place to meet! Parties are always more fun when you plan them with a best friend.

Having a sleepover with your best friend means sharing snacks, secrets, and LOLs!

Best friends can have pillow fights and
paint their toenails before snuggling into
their sleeping bags to watch a video.

Being with your best friend is always a treat,
and a great way to let her know that is to give
her something special.

It could be a daisy-chain necklace or something yummy you can share. No one knows better than best friends how to treat each other right!

Best friends love each other just the way they are, but it's still fun to give each other makeovers.

You can each find a "purr-fect" new look.

Try wearing a necklace, a bow, or even a tiara. One thing is for sure—having your best friend by your side is always your best accessory!

When you're feeling kind of slow and you're not sure if you can make it, your best friend can be your best cheerleader.

And even if you are the last to cross the finish line, your best friend won't leave you behind, because a best friend is always worth waiting for.

Find a shady spot and add a blanket, a buddy, and a basket of goodies. It's a best-friend picnic!

You might like tuna and she might like
roast beef, but you'll both love spending an
afternoon together spying cloud shapes in
the sky.

If you think going to the movies with your best friend is fun, why not try making a movie together?

Grab a costume and a camera and you can be a
star in your own backyard!

Best friends know that snacks always taste better when you share them.

Sharing a snack is always thoughtful, and it's part of what makes friendship so yummy!

Best friends love learning together, playing together, and eating together in the cafeteria.

Plus, best friends make the best study buddies!

A best friend can take you on a trip across the ocean or just a trip across town. Either way, traveling together is twice the fun.

And wherever you go together, friendship is always bound to be in style!

Everything's more fun when you share it with a best friend!